This book belongs to

_____

Walt Disney

VOLUME 8

DUMBO
AT BAT

WALT DISNEY FUN-TO-READ LIBRARY

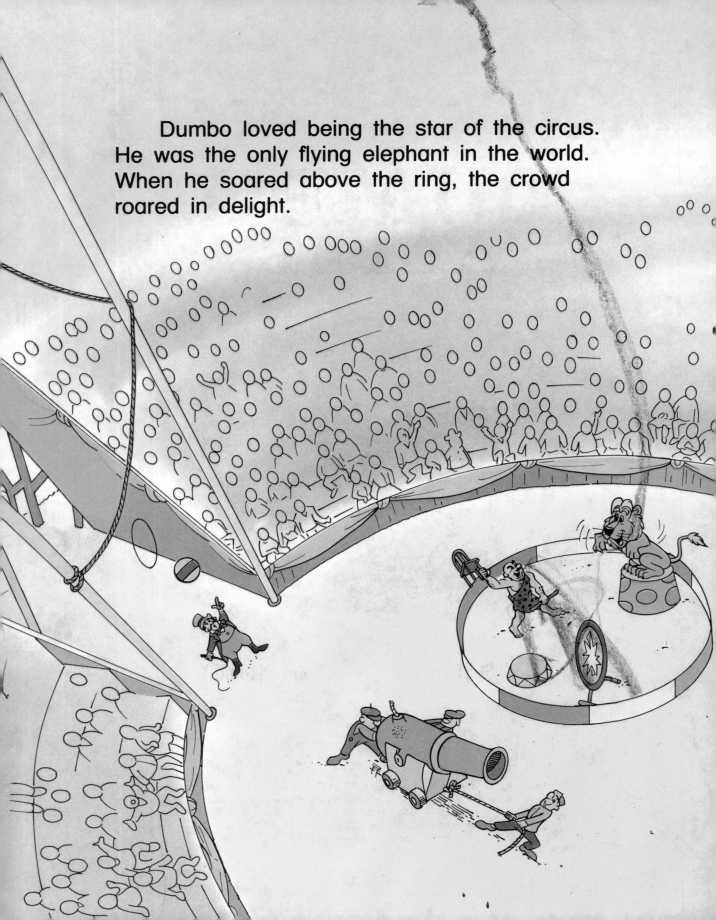

Dumbo loved being the star of the circus.
He was the only flying elephant in the world.
When he soared above the ring, the crowd
roared in delight.

He would circle high in the air.
"Go, Dumbo, go!" the crowd would cheer.
Dumbo was happy when he was flying.

One day after the show, the ringmaster called everyone together. "Now hear this," he said. "We are going to shut down for a few days. The circus wagons need to be painted."

"Oh, no," everyone cried.
"There will be nothing to do!" said Lion.
"Nothing at all," said one of the clowns.
Dumbo felt bad. No crowd would be
cheering, "Go, Dumbo, go!"

"Come on, everyone," said Timothy Mouse. "There <u>is</u> something to do. We can play baseball."

"Great idea!" said Lion.

"The clowns will play on one team. And
the animals will play on another team. We
are sure to win," the clowns said.

"Ha!" snorted Hippo. "Don't count on it.
We animals are pretty tough."

Dumbo looked worried. He did not know
how to play baseball.

The clowns got ready for the big game.
They practiced behind the cook's tent. They
threw balls very hard, and they caught them
every time. They hit balls very hard. They ran
fast around the field.

The animals practiced too. They played behind the big-top tent.

Lion threw the balls. Octopus caught them. Tiger hit the balls.

Dumbo watched them. He thought the animals were great.

Then it was Dumbo's turn.
He tried to throw the ball.
He tried to catch the ball.
Everyone watched.

"Things are bad," said Lion.
"Dumbo cannot play ball," Tiger whispered.
"What do we do now?" asked Bear.

At the end of the day, Dumbo heard
the other animals talking. They were talking
about him!

His team was going to lose, and it was
all because of him.

Timothy spoke to Dumbo. "You can learn to play ball. Just try it," he said. "Believe you can do it, and you will."

Dumbo was not so sure of that. And he cried himself to sleep that night.

When the next morning came, the animals practiced again. They all hit the ball. *Wham! Wham! Wham! Wham!*

Suddenly Bear asked, "Where is Dumbo?" Dumbo wasn't there.

"I'll get him," said Lion.
He knew just where to find him.
"You must get up," he said. "You
can play ball, my friend. Come. We will
teach you."

Dumbo tried to hit the ball.
"Go, Dumbo, go! Swing that bat!" the
animals cried.
Dumbo swung the bat—and missed!

Dumbo tried to run around the field. He
fell flat on his face.

"I just cannot play ball. I can't, I can't!"
he thought again and again.

The clowns looked on and laughed.

At last it was the day of the big game.
"We're going to win," called the clowns.
"Who says?" hooted the animals.

"We say," called the clowns. "Dumbo will help us win," they jeered. Then they all laughed.

"Giraffe, you catch the high balls," said Timothy. "Crocodile, you catch the low balls." Then he told everyone else what they should do.

He looked at Dumbo. "Well, maybe you can watch for a while. Then you will get the hang of it."

Dumbo was happy. As long as he did not play, his team would win.

"Play ball!" called the ringmaster.

The big game started.
The first clown at bat hit a home run.
The second clown hit one too.
"Hurray for us!" the clowns cheered.
"We're the greatest."

At last the animals came to bat. Bear
hit a home run. Lion hit a home run. So did
Crocodile and Ostrich. The animals were
winning 4 to 2.

"We are the best," they shouted.
Dumbo cheered.

They played all day. Neither team scored another run until the last inning. Then the clowns' best hitter came up to bat.

He hit the ball with a mighty *whack!* Giraffe tried to catch it. But he fell down. The clowns scored three more runs. They were winning, 5 to 4.

"Dumbo!" called Timothy. "Giraffe is hurt. You must take his place."

Dumbo shook his head. No! No! No!

"You must, Dumbo," said Timothy. "You can do it. Believe in yourself."

"Hurray!" shouted the clowns. "Here comes Dumbo. Now we know we will win the game!"

Dumbo took Giraffe's place.

With one out left, the next clown at bat
hit the ball toward Dumbo. Could Dumbo
catch it?

"Believe, Dumbo! Believe!" called Timothy.

Dumbo ran and ran. He jumped up high.
He caught the ball! The clowns were out.

"How did Dumbo catch that ball?" the clowns grumbled to each other.
Now it was the animals' last turn at bat.

The pitcher for the clowns threw the ball.
Bear struck out. So did Hippo. But Lion
hit the ball, and he ran to third base. The
animals had one last chance to win.

Now the game was up to Dumbo.
The pitcher threw the ball.
"Strike one!" called the ringmaster.
The pitcher threw the ball again.
Dumbo swung, but his ears got in the
way of the bat.
"Strike two!" called the ringmaster.

Timothy ran to Dumbo. He tied up his friend's ears. Then he whispered once again, "Believe, Dumbo! Believe!"

The clown threw the ball again.
This time Dumbo hit it. *Wham!*
"Run, Dumbo, run," called the animals.

"Believe in yourself," called Timothy. "You can do it, Dumbo. Run!"

"Maybe I can," Dumbo thought.

He passed first base and kept on running. Lion ran to home plate. Now the score was 5 to 5!

Dumbo had hit the ball so hard that the clowns could not stop it. They scrambled all around the field.

"Dum-bo, Dum-bo," called the animals. "Go, go, go."

Finally a clown picked up the ball.
But Dumbo was on his way past second
base. "I think I can," he thought.

He passed third base. "I <u>know</u> I can," he said to himself.

The clown threw the ball to the catcher at home plate.

"Slide, Dumbo, slide," the animals called.

And Dumbo did! He slid right under the catcher's arm!

"Safe!" called the ringmaster.

Dumbo smiled. "I did it," he thought. "I did it!"

"We won, we won!" the animals cheered. "Hurray for Dumbo!"

"How did he do it?" the clowns asked each other. "Yesterday he could not catch or hit."

Timothy smiled. He knew what had happened. "At last Dumbo believed in himself," he said. "That's the only answer."

Dumbo was happy. Once again he was the star of the day. And now he knew he could . . . PLAY BALL!